THE VANISHING VAMPIRE

Look for these books in the
Clue™ series:

Clue™

THE VANISHING VAMPIRE

Book created by A. E. Parker

Written by Marie Jacks

Based on characters from the Parker Brothers® game

A Creative Media Applications Production

SCHOLASTIC INC.
New York Toronto London Auckland Sydney

Special thanks to: Susan Nash, Laura Millhollin, Maureen Taxter, Jean Feiwel, Ellie Berger, Craig Walker, Greg Holch, Dona Smith, Kim Williams, Nancy Smith, John Simko, David Tommasino, Jennifer Presant, and Elizabeth Parisi.

ISBN 0-590-13742-5

Copyright © 1997 by Hasbro, Inc. All rights reserved. Published by Scholastic Inc. by arrangement with Parker Brothers, a division of Hasbro, Inc. Clue® is a registered trademark of Hasbro, Inc., for its detective game equipment.

12 11 10 9 8 7 6 5 4 3 2 1   7 8 9/9 0 1 2/0

Printed in the U.S.A.   40

First Scholastic printing, January 1997

Contents

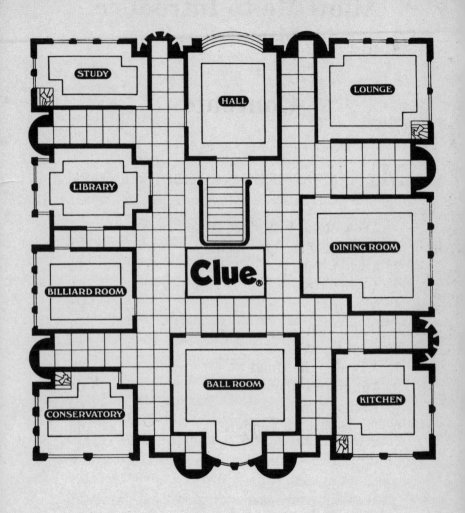

Allow Me to Introduce Myself . . .

My NAME IS REGINALD BODDY, AND I'M happy to welcome you to my mansion. You have a frightfully fun weekend in store for you.

You're probably shocked to see me standing here, alive and well. After all, not long ago my maid killed me. She has such a wacky sense of humor!

Let me explain what happened. When Mrs. White tried to murder me, we were in the Kitchen. Mrs. White accidentally picked up a banana instead of the Revolver. When she thought she was squeezing the trigger, she actually squeezed the banana, making the inside shoot from the peel and hit me splat in the middle of the forehead. I was momentarily stunned. Soon, however, I got up and slipped away.

Mrs. White sure made a monkey out of me. I'll never find bananas apeeling again. Now, however, I want to ask you a favor. Would you mind staying on your toes this weekend and watching for signs

1

of grisly crimes in the making? My guests have such zest for life that it sometimes makes them lie, cheat, steal, and even commit murder. They don't mean anything by it!

There are six suspects you'll have to keep an eye on. (I myself will never be a suspect, of course!) After each mystery, I'll provide you with a list of rooms, suspects, and weapons to help you keep track of whodunit. The six suspects are:

Mrs. White: My faithful maid. Unfortunately, she was maid to be a crook.

Mr. Green: His name gives a clue to his main interest. So do his aliases: Mr. Money, Mr. Banks, Mr. Silver, and Mr. Gold. I think you get the picture.

Mrs. Peacock: When it comes to manners, this lady wrote the book. In fact, she wrote *all* of them.

Colonel Mustard: His motto is, "I challenge you to a duel!" He says it all the time. As you can imagine, he keeps things lively that way.

Miss Scarlet: This lovely lady loves to flirt. But if you flirt back, you're flirting with danger. And of course, her favorite color is red.

Professor Plum: What can I say about the professor? It doesn't matter, because he'll forget whatever I say immediately.

*   *   *

2

I can't tell you how glad I am that you're here to help watch over things. Now I can rest in peace. Say, isn't it awfully quiet in here? That is not a good sign. I'd better go and check on my guests. Let's hope they're all still alive.

1.
Something to Talk About

"INTO THE DINING ROOM, EVERYONE!" Mr. Boddy said brightly. "Hurry up, now. Scoot! Scoot! Come along, Mrs. White!"

"I don't like that coot telling me to scoot," Mrs. White grumbled to herself.

After the guests had all gone into the Dining Room, they gazed at Mr. Boddy expectantly. "I have gathered you all here because I have noticed that we haven't had a conversation lately," Mr. Boddy told them. "In fact, everyone wanders around talking loudly to themselves. Now that you've taken to wearing white coats, too, you're scaring the neighbors."

"At least when I talk to myself, I have someone witty to talk to," objected Miss Scarlet.

"I've only challenged *myself* to a duel a few times," said Colonel Mustard.

"The replies are never rude," said Mrs. Peacock.

"I always learn something new," said Mr. Green.

"I always love the gossip," said Mrs. White. "And I never talk behind my own back."

4

"I never mind if I forget what I've said," added Professor Plum. "At least, if I remember correctly."

"Come, come, now." Mr. Boddy shook his head. "It will be much better to talk to each other." He pulled out one of the six chairs at the circular table and Miss Scarlet sat down. "Ladies and gentlemen, would you please alternate your seats?" Mr. Boddy asked politely. "I think that will make the conversation livelier."

"Boy, girl, boy, girl," said a male guest with a wink as he took a seat on Miss Scarlet's left. Another male guest started to sit down next to him. "Have you forgotten Mr. Boddy's request already?" thundered the first male guest. "I'll challenge you to a duel if you sit in that chair!

"Don't be such a grouch. I just forgot," whispered the second male guest under his breath as he ran to sit by Miss Scarlet.

As two more guests took their seats, Mr. Boddy spotted Mrs. White trying to sneak out the window. He grabbed her by the hem of her white coat, and dragged her back inside. Reluctantly, she took a seat.

Mr. Boddy stood near the door, in case anyone tried to make a run for it. "Let the conversation begin!" he prompted.

The guests looked at each other in silence. Minute after minute ticked by. Everyone sighed again and again until the room sounded like a wind tunnel or the seashore at high tide in the middle of a hurricane.

"Stop that!" yelled Mr. Boddy at the top of his lungs. Everyone stopped sighing and listened. "Let's go around the table in a clockwise direction," he said. "Each person should take a turn making a comment." He nodded to the woman to the left of Colonel Mustard. "Please start."

The only sound in the room was the ticking of the clock. The woman developed a nervous tic. Her face grew red with embarrassment. *It's rude to keep everyone waiting*, she thought in a panic.

"It's nice we're having weather," she stammered finally. Her face grew redder as she realized her mistake. "I mean, it's nice weather we're having."

Ploink! A hailstone bounced off the window, causing them all to jump about three feet in the air and howl in pain as they landed. "Oh dear, the weather isn't nice at all," the woman fretted. Her face was now a frightening shade of deep magenta.

"Your turn is up!" bellowed the guest next to her. "It's my turn." He quickly realized that he had spoken too soon, because he didn't have anything to say at all. Finally, he looked out the window, where the gale was so strong it was ripping the trees out by the roots and tossing them around the lawn like Ping-Pong balls.

"The sun will come out tomorrow." The guest nodded his head wisely.

"Bet your bottom hundred-dollar-bill," said the next guest in agreement.

The guest whose turn was next forgot what he was going to say. Everyone stared at him, and he grew so self-conscious that the hair stood straight up on his head. Finally he looked at the guest on his left and sang out, "You say po-tay-to, and I say po-tah-to pancake."

Your head looks like one, thought the guest on his left, but she did as he said and repeated, "Po-tay-to." Then she turned to the guest next to her and sang, "You say to-may-to, and I say to-mah-to catsup," belting it out as if she were the star of a Broadway musical.

The guest on her left winced at the sound. "To-may-to," he repeated. Then he slapped his forehead with his hand. "Let's call the whole thing off!" he roared.

"No, no, no, no!" insisted Mr. Boddy. Please co-operate and try harder," he urged. "Let's start over and go around the table again. Go ahead," he nodded to the woman who started off the first time.

Once again, her mind was a blank. It was her worst nightmare, because she thought she was being rude. The pressure caused beads of perspiration to stand out on her forehead.

"Piffle!" she blurted out at last.

The next guest scowled. "Oopsy daisy,'" he said gruffly.

"Whoops!" said the next guest, sticking her tongue out at him.

"I say po-tah-to pancake," said the guest to her left.

"Fiddle-dee-dee, you already said that," said the female guest whose turn was next. She tapped her red nails on the table.

"Zounds!" The male guest next to her leaped to his feet. "This talk was ridiculous. I challenge every one of you to a duel!"

"Great!" The other guests cried in unison. They were all so bored and frustrated that they were seething with rage inside.

Within seconds they had all jumped out of their chairs and started swinging at each other, while Mr. Boddy cringed in a corner. In order to end the brawl, he had to call the whole thing off.

Later that night . . .

Later that night, when the mansion was dark, the guests were still steamed up. They paced the floor and brooded about how to kill each other off. Then one by one, they started to carry out their plans.

"I'll slice your head like a to-may-to," said a guest as he sneaked up behind another in the Study.

But the other guest was too quick for him, and leaped up and whacked him on the noggin, screeching, "I'll thump your head until it's to-mah-to catsup."

"Zounds," groaned the guest as he slumped to the floor. Grinning gleefully, the other guest raced toward the Ball Room, planning to conk someone else on the head.

When the guest reached the Ball Room, she found it was empty — or at least that's what she thought. Another guest hiding behind the door sprang out and choked her with the Rope.

"Whoops!" said the guest with the Rope as her victim fell to the floor. She giggled so hard that she didn't hear another guest sneak up behind her.

"One po-tah-to, two po-tah-to," he cried as he struck her twice with the Wrench. The guest with the Rope slumped to the floor. An instant later, the Revolver went off.

"Oopsy daisy!" laughed the guest who had fired the shot. The guest with the Wrench joined the guest with the Rope and other guest on the Ball Room floor.

The guest with the Revolver chuckled and clapped his hands together as he danced out of the Ball Room.

As soon as the laughing guest with the Revolver had gone on his way, one of the guests on the Ball Room floor revived, grabbed a weapon, and went on the prowl.

Meanwhile, another angry guest was creeping through the mansion. When the guest with the Revolver whizzed by her, laughing, she hit him over the head with the Candlestick. "Piffle!" she said. Then she walked into the Conservatory, on the lookout for another victim.

Suddenly, the guest who had revived ran toward her. "Piffle!" shrieked the guest with the Candlestick in surprise. Then she ran forward, swinging her weapon over her head.

At the last minute, the other guest stepped aside and used a weapon to *thwonk!* the guest with the Candlestick on the head.

"Piffle!" cried the guest as she fell to the floor.

The guest standing over her looked down with satisfaction and whispered, "You already said that."

WHICH GUEST WAS THE LAST ONE STANDING?

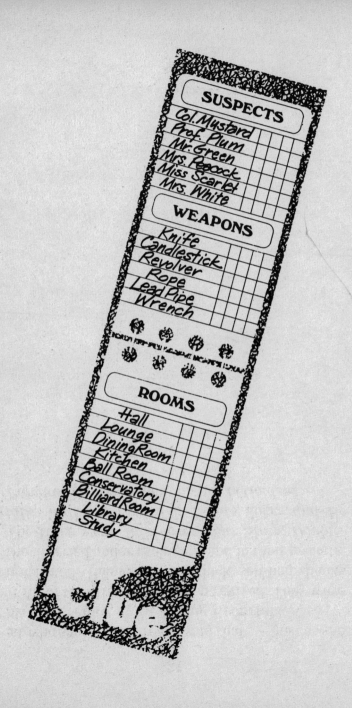

let who said, "You already said that" — just as she had said before, at the Dining Room table.

All of the other guests soon revived. They were unharmed, thanks to the thick self-help books they carried under their caps and in their pockets. The titles were *Talking in Your Sleep*, *Double-talk*, *Walkie-talkies*, *Tell Potato Jokes and Be Popular at Parties*, and *Silence Is Golden*.

SOLUTION

MISS SCARLET in the CONSERVATORY with the LEAD PIPE

We know that Miss Scarlet sat down at the table first. The duel-happy gentleman who sat next to her on her left had to be Colonel Mustard. Then forgetful Professor Plum sat on Scarlet's right. The lady next to Colonel Mustard who panicked at the thought of being rude was Mrs. Peacock. The guest who sat next to her had to be a male, so it was Mr. Green. Mrs. White took the seat between Green and Plum.

By keeping track of what the guests say as they take their turns clockwise around the table, we can figure out who says what later.

Colonel Mustard planned to use the Knife to slice Miss Scarlet's head like a to-may-to. Instead, she thumped his head as if it was a to-mah-to. Miss Scarlet was choked with the Rope by Mrs. White who said, "Whoops!" Then Mrs. White was struck by the guest who said "po-tah-to pancake" — Professor Plum. Mr. Green said, "Oopsy daisy," as he shot Plum with the Revolver. Mrs. Peacock said "Piffle!" after she knocked Green out with the Candlestick. Then she was attacked by another guest who had revived. That guest was Miss Scar-

2.
A Dog's Tale

ONE AFTERNOON, WHEN THE GUESTS were sitting in the Conservatory and plotting which of Mr. Boddy's treasures to steal next, Mr. Boddy came in holding a scruffy-looking puppy with strange spots shaped like dollar signs. "I have a new pet," he announced. "This mutt's name is Jeff. His full name is Jeff the Wonder Puppy."

"Did you find him in a pup tent?" snickered Miss Scarlet.

"That was a catty remark," sniffed the proper Mrs. Peacock.

"I think you're barking up the wrong tree," snapped Mr. Green.

"Such an ordinary dog wouldn't fetch much of a price," sneered Mrs. White.

"He doesn't look like such a hot dog," said Professor Plum snidely.

"*Wiener* you going to tell us about that dog?" snarled Colonel Mustard.

"I'd tell you if you would all stop hounding me," Mr. Boddy said impatiently.

"Jeff is worth one million dollars," Mr. Boddy

continued. The room got so quiet that you could hear a pin drop. "You see, he is a famous animal motion picture star."

"What pictures was he in?" the guests all asked at once.

Mr. Boddy smiled proudly. "He just starred in *The Life of Labrador Dali*, the movie about the dog that was a surrealist painter."

There was a chorus of "Wow!" and "Bow-wow!" None of the guests had seen *The Life of Labrador Dali*, but they knew the picture had made a lot of money. Whoever owned Jeff was sure to make a bundle on his next picture.

Mr. Boddy went on and on, bragging about the puppy. While Mr. Boddy was talking, all of the guests stuffed weapons in their pockets. Now they were doggone sure which one of Mr. Boddy's treasures they wanted to steal next.

Later that night . . .

Later that night, all the guests crept around the mansion, looking for the puppy. One guest ventured toward the Conservatory, holding the Lead Pipe in one hand and sweeping with the other. "I can't miss a chance to get a jump on the next day's chores," whispered the guest, "just in case I don't get the dog."

Another guest overheard this. "That dog will be mine," he said furiously as he attacked the first

15

guest with the Candlestick and took the Lead Pipe.

"Why did I do that?" he asked himself a moment later as he looked at the other guest lying on the floor. In all the excitement, he forgot what he wanted to steal, and why he was holding the Lead Pipe and the Candlestick. He racked his brain, but it was no use. He couldn't remember. The guest gave up, went to bed, and slept soundly through the night.

No sooner had he left when another guest crept into the Kitchen and spied the dog snoozing in a corner. She tiptoed over and started to tie up the puppy with the Rope, nearly breaking a red nail in the process.

"Now that I've decided to flee with you, I hope you don't have any fleas," she said.

Jeff the Wonder Puppy woke up and immediately sensed that he was being stolen. He decided to nip the situation in the bud by nipping the thief in the shins.

"Aarrgh!" shrieked the thief. She jumped so high in the air that she banged her head on the ceiling and, like the first guest, was knocked out for the night.

The dog raced into the Hall. Another guest spotted the spotted dog and ran after him. Jeff was fast, though, and he nearly got away.

Then the guest fired a shot into the air with the Revolver. Startled and scared, Jeff stopped in his tracks. The guest grabbed him, but then got worried.

"What if the shot awakened Boddy?" he whispered. "If he catches me, I'll be in the doghouse."

Unwilling to risk getting caught, the thief let the dog go. The guest went to bed and spent the rest of the night cowering under the covers.

Soon another guest spotted the spotted dog as it scampered into the Lounge. Clutching the Wrench, the guest hurried after the dog, full of dignity and purpose. However, the guest tripped over the dog, who was lounging on the floor of the Lounge. The guest went flying. After doing three cartwheels, two handsprings, and four somersaults, the guest landed on the floor and got knocked out in the process.

An hour went by. By then, the puppy had curled up in the Library and gone to sleep, snoring like a freight train. The noise alerted a guest to his whereabouts.

"You're all pupped out — I mean, pooped out," chuckled the guest, tiptoeing over to the puppy. She opened a jar and began spreading something on the dog with a weapon. "This will disguise those dollar-sign shaped spots so that you won't be spotted as a hot dog — a stolen dog, that is," whispered the guest.

Then the guest heard footsteps. "What's going on there?" someone called.

The guest recognized Mr. Boddy's voice, and

17

jumped away from the dog. By the time Mr. Boddy reached the Library, the guest, the jar, and the weapon were gone. Mr. Boddy took the dog to his room and locked the door.

The next morning . . .

The next morning, when the guests were all gathered at breakfast, Mr. Boddy confronted them, holding the dog in his arms. "I've got a bone to pick with you," he said, while the dog growled at all of the guests. "I'll bet whoever did this was trying to steal my dog. Now I'll have to take the poor pooch to a dogtor."

Mrs. White's mouth dropped open when she saw the dog. "Why, that dog is covered with yellow slime!"

"The poor dog is covered with yellow paint!" exclaimed Professor Plum.

"Ugh, he's covered with golden goo," said Miss Scarlet.

"It's no yolk," said Mr. Green, laughing at his own joke.

"That dog is covered with mustard!" exclaimed Mrs. Peacock. The others eyed Colonel Mustard, who glared at Mrs. Peacock.

WHO YELLOWED THE DOG?/WITH WHAT WEAPON?

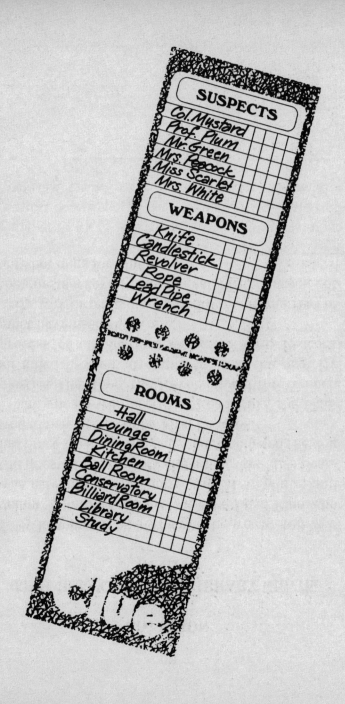

SOLUTION

MRS. PEACOCK in the LIBRARY with the KNIFE

By keeping track of the guests, we can tell who yellowed Jeff. The guest with the Lead Pipe who was catching up on chores was Mrs. White, and the guest who nearly broke a nail was Miss Scarlet. Since we know the guest who yellowed the dog was female, it has to be Mrs. Peacock.

The guests who used the Lead Pipe, the Candlestick, the Rope, the Revolver, and the Wrench all failed in their attempts to steal the dog. By process of elimination, we know Mrs. Peacock must have used the Knife.

By way of punishment Boddy made the rest of the guests a seven-course meal. Mrs. Peacock got only hot dogs for dinner.

3.
A Nutty Day

MR. BODDY INVITED HIS GUESTS INTO the Lounge, where there was a huge bowl of peanuts on the table.

Mrs. White stood beside Mr. Boddy and eyed him suspiciously. "What's going on here?" she asked.

"I want to play a game," he said. "I'm going to draw numbers out of this hat and tell each one of you how many peanuts to take. We'll play until all the peanuts are gone. The person with the most peanuts wins."

"You want us to play for peanuts? Have you gone off your nut?" asked Mr. Green.

"Shell out some dough," said Miss Scarlet.

"Cashew! Cashew!" sneezed Mrs. Peacock, who then apologized for being so rude as to sneeze.

"You're right to sneeze at playing for peanuts," said Colonel Mustard.

"I think you've gone plum nuts," said Professor Plum.

"Nuts to you, Boddy," said Mrs. White. "I refuse to play."

"Very well, Mrs. White. You can hand out the nuts to the guests as I draw the numbers. I insist that everyone else play."

Mrs. White smiled smugly. Everyone else groaned.

"I almost forgot to mention the prize I will award to the person who gets the most nuts," said Boddy. He held up a solid gold peanut worth several thousand dollars.

All of the guests suddenly took an interest in the game. "I'd love to put that in my trunk," shouted Colonel Mustard. "How much is it worth, anyway?"

"Tusk, tusk," said Mrs. Peacock. "You're too nosy, Colonel."

"I'll play after all," said Mrs. White. But, to teach her a lesson about being grumpy, Mr. Boddy refused to let her play.

"The drawing will be a secret," Mr. Boddy continued, while Mrs. White made faces at his back. "I won't call out the numbers. I'll simply hand the correct number of nuts to Mrs. White for her to distribute to each of you."

Mr. Boddy looked over his shoulder and smiled at Mrs. White. She grinned, then scowled as soon as Mr. Boddy looked away.

"Please don't gloat or whine about how many nuts you get. Keep the totals to yourselves," Mr. Boddy told his guests.

"A nut bag for a nutbag," said Mrs. White as Mrs. Peacock picked up her bag.

"How rude!" sputtered Mrs. Peacock. "What acorny thing to say."

"You shouldn't have a bag for your nuts," said Green to Mustard. "You should put yours in a case."

Colonel Mustard looked puzzled.

"A nut case for a nutcase," Green explained with a chuckle.

"I challenge you to a duel!" roared the Colonel.

Mr. Boddy calmed him down. "We don't have time, Colonel. I want to get the game started."

Boddy quieted all the guests and they began to play.

After the fourth round, Scarlet had one hundred nuts, Plum had half as many, Mustard had half as many as Plum, Peacock had six more than Plum, and Green had eight more than Mustard.

During the fifth round, Scarlet got ten more nuts and Plum doubled his total. Mustard tripled his total, then accidentally dropped three which rolled under the couch. Mrs. Peacock got twenty more, but lost ten when Mustard stole them from her when she wasn't looking. Mr. Green got thirty more, and grabbed Mustard's nuts that had rolled under the couch.

Before they went into the sixth round, Mrs. White, who was seething that she couldn't compete for the prize, switched off the lights. In the dark she ran around grabbing peanuts from the guests and stuffing them in her pockets. When her pockets were full she stuffed them in her mouth. She managed to steal thirty from Scarlet, twenty from Plum, twelve from Mustard, and six each from Peacock and Green. Then she bumped into Miss Scarlet. Five more nuts fell from Miss Scarlet's bag, and Mrs. White managed to grab those, too.

Then Mr. Boddy switched the lights back on. He announced that the game was over, and everyone should count how many peanuts they had. While he was counting, Professor Plum forgot what he was doing for a few minutes and ate six of his peanuts.

WHO WON THE SOLID GOLD PEANUT?

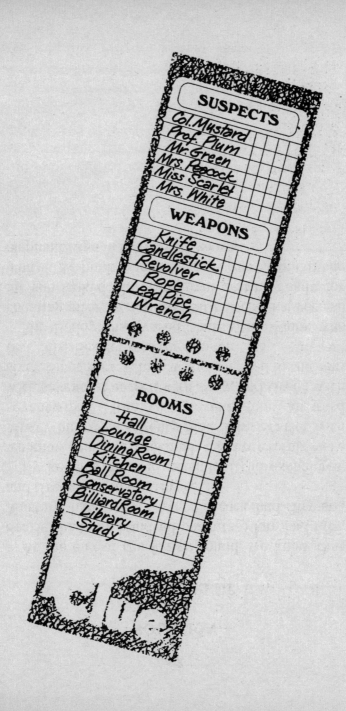

SOLUTION

MISS SCARLET

At the end of the fourth round, we know that Scarlet had one hundred peanuts, Plum had fifty, Mustard had twenty-five, Peacock had fifty-six, and Green had thirty-three.

By keeping careful account of the exchanges, we know that after the final round the totals were Mrs. White with seventy-nine, Miss Scarlet with seventy-five, Plum with seventy-four, Mustard with seventy, Peacock with sixty, and Green with sixty. Since Mrs. White wasn't allowed in the contest, Miss Scarlet was the winner.

Mr. Boddy discovered that Mrs. White was cheating after he noticed that her cheeks were so fat she looked like a squirrel getting ready for winter. As punishment he made her clean out the elephant cage in his private zoo.

4.
Ham It Up

MR. BODDY HAD GATHERED HIS GUESTS in the dining room for the unveiling of his latest treasure. He pulled the velvet cloth off with a flourish to reveal what looked like an ordinary set of false teeth.

The guests weren't impressed. "Tell the tooth, Boddy — I mean, the truth," said Mr. Green. "What is so special about that ordinary set of choppers?"

Boddy explained that it wasn't an ordinary pair of false teeth at all. It was really a valuable sculpture done by the famous artist Georgia O'Teeth before she went on to paint pictures of cow skulls and flowers. Sure enough, the sculpture bore the signature, *Georgia O'Teeth*.

"Hmm," said Colonel Mustard, popping one of his favorite candies — a lime gumdrop — into his mouth.

"These teeth are really valuable," said Mr. Boddy. "They're worth a lot of money." Then he said. "They're worth a lot of money," again. Then he said it again.

"You've certainly drilled it into us," said Mrs. White.

"All right, then," Mr. Boddy clapped his hands. "I can't wait to have a party to celebrate my latest acquisition. Since we all use teeth to chew, I've decided to have a costume party, and all my guests should come dressed as their favorite foods."

"What a great idea!" squealed the guests. While they were squealing, they were thinking about stealing — stealing the teeth. Still squealing, they snuck weapons into their pockets.

Mr. Green took the Lead Pipe.

Mrs. White took the Rope.

Professor Plum took the Revolver.

The other guests each chose one of the remaining weapons.

At the party in the Dining Room, Boddy examined their costumes one by one. Mr. Green was dressed in a pink costume that was covered with cloves. Mr. Boddy didn't know what it was until Green said, "Oink! Oink!" Then he realized Green was a ham.

Mrs. White was in a round, fat orange costume — an orange.

Miss Scarlet was dressed in red and white swirls — a candy cane.

When the others saw Plum's white costume with the yellow circle, Mr. Boddy joked that he certainly was scrambled. "Don't egg them on," Plum begged Boddy. He was, of course, an egg.

Then Mr. Boddy saw someone approaching dressed in brown, with huge earmuffs that looked like rolls. At first he thought it was his niece, Patty. It was actually Mrs. Peacock, dressed as a hamburger.

While they waited for the last guest, Mr. Boddy suddenly remembered that he had an appointment. "I have to leave immediately," he told his guests. "Please carry on without me. I'll be back as soon as I can."

The guests couldn't believe their good fortune. "Good-bye!" they called. "Don't worry about us. Take your time!"

While the other guests were busy saying good-bye to Boddy, a guest in a green costume wrenched the teeth from the table with the Wrench and raced into the Kitchen. The guest who was dressed as an egg spied the theft. The egg charged after the thief, calling "Stop or I'll shoot!" and fired the Revolver. But the thief didn't stop and continued running into the Ball Room.

Meanwhile . . .

Meanwhile, one of the remaining guests noticed that the teeth were missing. "I'm missing teeth!" he cried. He and the other guests gave chase.

The candy cane caught up to the egg, hit him on the head with the Candlestick, and kept on running after the guest in green.

29

In the Conservatory, the candy cane was caught around the neck by the orange with the Rope. The candy cane fell choking to the floor. The orange nearly caught up with the guest in green in the Billiard Room, but another guest attacked her with a Knife. The orange fell to the floor, clutching her chest.

The guest with the Knife attacked the one with the green costume and got away with the teeth.

WHO STOLE THE FALSE TEETH?

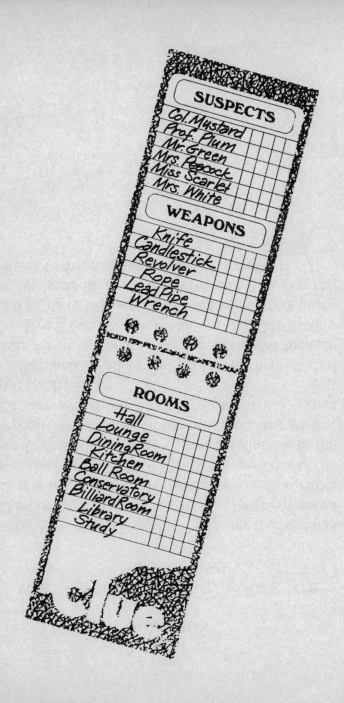

SOLUTION

MRS. PEACOCK in the BILLIARD ROOM
with the KNIFE

By process of elimination, we know that Colonel Mustard was the thief in green — he was dressed as a lime gumdrop. The first guest to give chase was the egg (Professor Plum), the second was the candy cane (Miss Scarlet), and the third was the orange (Mrs. White). Of the two remaining guests, Mr. Green had the Lead Pipe and Mrs. Peacock had the Knife.

Fortunately, all of the guests were protected from harm by their costumes. But unfortunately for Mrs. Peacock, she found out that Mr. Boddy had actually just signed the famous artist's name to his grandfather's old false teeth to get the guests to dress up for the costume party.

5.
Door Prize

"**I** HAVE AN INTERESTING TASK FOR YOU all to do," Mr. Boddy told his guests, who were assembled in the Ball Room.

The guests groaned.

"All of the doors in the mansion need painting. I'd like you all to do it." Mr. Boddy smiled, quite pleased with himself for thinking of the project.

The guests groaned again.

"Do you think I'm a doormat?" roared Mr. Green.

"I shutter to think!" thundered Colonel Mustard. "I'll challenge you to a duel!" he said to Mr. Boddy.

"Oh, hush up," said Miss Scarlet impatiently. Then she turned to Mr. Boddy. "Can't you get the doorman to do it?" she asked.

"Door*person*," corrected Mrs. Peacock.

"I haven't got one," said Boddy. "You won't want to be behind the door when you find out that I'm offering a prize to the person who paints the most doors."

"Is it a door prize?" asked Professor Plum.

"Well, in a way, yes," Boddy replied.

"We can all hobknob while we paint," said Mrs. Peacock.

"What an adoorable comment," sniffed Professor Plum.

"Please, everyone, be quiet," Boddy said. "Let's get started right away. There will be a time limit, so you must work quickly. The one who has painted the most doors when I announce that the time is up wins the prize. Now step right up and get your paints, brushes, hats, and smocks."

Miss Scarlet picked up the red can of paint with the Revolver.

Mrs. White picked up the white can of paint with the Wrench.

Mr. Green grabbed the green paint can with the Knife.

Colonel Mustard took the yellow can with the Rope.

Mrs. Peacock picked up the blue can of paint ever so properly with the Lead Pipe.

Professor Plum grabbed the can of purple paint with the Candlestick.

"There are a lot of doors in this mansion," White said sourly, when all the guests had picked up their paint. "There is a door in the Study, a door in the Lounge, a door in the Kitchen, and a door in the Conservatory. The Hall, Dining Room, Billiard Room, and Library all have two doors. The Ball Room has four."

"I had a four-door once," said Plum. "It was a great little car."

The others shushed him.

"Your count was accurate, Mrs. White," said Boddy. "But you only thought of the doors used for entrance and exit. There are more doors inside the rooms."

"That's right," said Mrs. Peacock. "There is a door inside the Study, and a door inside the Kitchen."

"There are three inside the Conservatory, said Plum.

"There is a door inside the Billiard Room," said Mustard.

"There is a door inside the Lounge," said Green.

"Knock on wood, I think that's all the doors there are," said Mr. Boddy. He clapped his hands together. "Now get started, everyone!" he said.

Professor Plum dashed into the Conservatory, Mrs. White ran to the Dining Room, Miss Scarlet raced to the Ball Room, Mr. Green hurried to the Billiard Room, Mrs. Peacock went to the Study, and Colonel Mustard to the Kitchen.

Miss Scarlet had painted one door when Mustard came charging into the room wearing a cowboy outfit instead of a painting smock. He was already done with the doors in the Kitchen, and he meant to finish the doors in the Ball Room. He lassoed Scarlet with the Rope, shouting, "Yippee-ai-o-kai-yay!" and sent her flying out of the room, paint can in hand.

Mrs. Peacock painted two doors in the Study and one in the Hall. She was congratulating herself on a job properly done when the guest who had just painted the doors in the Dining Room hit her on the head with the Wrench. "Mind your manners," she said as Mrs. Peacock fell to the floor. The guest took her weapon and painted the other door in the Hall.

Meanwhile . . .

Meanwhile, after painting the remaining doors in the Ball Room, the guest with the Rope went into the Billiard Room. He chuckled when he saw there was a door left unpainted, but then was attacked by the guest who was already there with the Knife. "Happy trails," said the guest with the Knife, who then finished the last door in the Billiard Room, and went into the Library.

Before the guest with the Knife could paint any more doors, he was conked on the head with the Lead Pipe. "Pipe down," said the guest with a sneer. Then the guest took his weapon from him and finished the doors in the Library.

The guest who had been lassoed in the Ball Room painted all of the doors in the Lounge, then crept into the Library and attacked the guest who had just finished painting the doors. "Take that!" she said as she fired the Revolver. The other guest fell to the floor, and the guest with the Revolver painted both doors over with her own color.

Meanwhile . . .

Meanwhile the guest in the Conservatory was scratching his head because he couldn't find one of the doors. "When is a door not a door?" he mumbled. Just as he remembered there was one less door than he had thought, a bullet came zinging into the room, sending him crashing to the floor.

"A door is not a door when it's ajar," hissed the guest who fired the Revolver. "These doors are mine, and I'll paint them my own color!"

The guest had done just that when Mr. Boddy announced, "Time is up!"

WHO PAINTED THE MOST DOORS AND WON THE PRIZE?

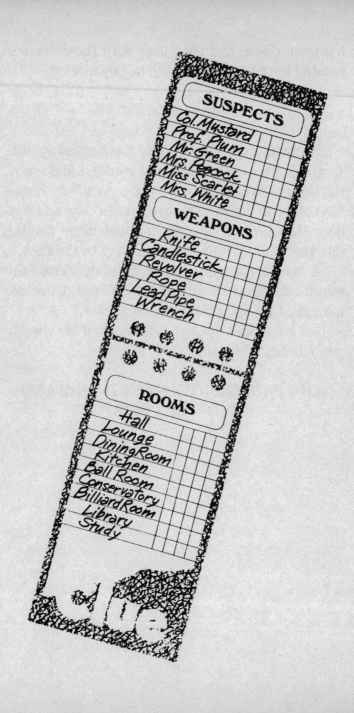

SOLUTION

MISS SCARLET

By keeping track of how many doors there were in each room, we know that Mrs. White started off with two doors in the Dining Room. Mrs. Peacock started off with two doors in the Study and one in the Hall before she was attacked. Mrs. White took her weapon, the Lead Pipe, and painted the other door in the Hall.

Miss Scarlet painted one door in the Ball Room before Colonel Mustard lassoed her and painted the other three. Mr. Green painted the doors in the Billiard Room, and also put Colonel Mustard out of commission with the Knife. Then Mr. Green was conked on the head in the Library with the Lead Pipe, the weapon Mrs. White had taken from Mrs. Peacock. Mrs. White then painted all the doors in the Library. But after Miss Scarlet attacked Mrs. White with the Revolver, she repainted all the doors with her own color. She then attacked Professor Plum in the Conservatory, and painted his doors her color as well. In the end Plum got credit for no doors, White got credit for three, Scarlet painted eight, Green did three, Peacock did three, and Mustard painted five.

All of the guests were unharmed. Since he knew their greedy nature, Mr. Boddy had made sure the hats and smocks he gave them were slashproof, crashproof, and bulletproof.

In the end, Boddy gave everyone a prize, but the guests weren't too thrilled with it. It was bars of soap to clean the paint off their hands.

6.
Food Fight

"LUNCHEON IS SERVED," MRS. WHITE screeched in a voice that sounded like chalk being dragged across a blackboard. She opened the door to the Dining Room.

Inside the Dining Room, a splendid buffet was laid out on a long table. At the head of the table was a basket of fruit and the appetizers, followed by baskets of rolls. Next to the rolls were potatoes — scalloped, mashed, and baked, in that order. Next to the baked potatoes were a plate of ham and a whole roast turkey, with a platter of roast beef in between. Next to the turkey was a huge gravy boat filled with gravy. Then came the vegetable section, with bowls of broccoli, spinach, and carrots in that order. Finally came the desserts — first the angel food cake, and then the chocolate cake.

"Okay, get it yourselves," Mrs. White said, scowling. Then she saw that Mr. Boddy was close by, and added, "I mean, please help yourselves."

"It looks lovely, Mrs. White," Mr. Boddy told her. "Please join the others for lunch."

"Don't do me any favors," Mrs. White hissed under her breath. Then she said, "Thanks a bunch."

"Go ahead, help yourselves," Mr. Boddy urged his guests.

The words were barely out of his mouth when the guests stampeded toward the table like a herd of cattle at roundup time. They jostled each other as they got in line.

"I'm first, and I'll challenge anyone who tries to get ahead of me to a duel," said a male guest. He changed his mind when Scarlet glared at him. "Anyone, that is, except a lady," he stammered.

The three ladies quickly hurried to the front of the line. "Age before beauty," said one of them as another cut in front of her.

"How rude!" sputtered the other guest. Then she retorted, "Pearls before swine."

"Listen, 'Pearl,'" said the third female guest. "You aren't too prim and proper to cut in line, I see. Well, don't try that with me." Then the third female guest stepped to the head of the line.

The two male guests behind Mustard exchanged angry looks. "You'll have more than ring-around-the-collar if you try to cut in front of me," said one of them. "I'll wring your purple-collared neck."

The guest with the purple collar stepped to the end of the line. He grabbed an apple from the fruit basket and chucked it at the guest who had threatened to wring his neck, but it bounced off his head and he didn't feel a thing.

By the time he reached the appetizers, Colonel Mustard decided he wasn't going to be chivalrous when he was hungry. "Let me pass or I'll challenge you all to a duel!" he said as he jumped to the head of the line.

This routine of challenging everyone to a duel all the time is getting to be a bore, thought the female guest directly behind him. She ladled a few healthy spoonfuls of scalloped potatoes down his back. "Today, lunch is on you," she chuckled.

The guest realized that what she said was true. He was wearing lunch on his back. Too sticky and uncomfortable to think of dueling, the guest at the head of the line left to go and get cleaned up.

Meanwhile, a guest with long red nails was helping herself to mashed potatoes. "I just love mashed po-tay-toes," she whispered as she piled them on her plate.

"I just love baked po-tah-toes," said Professor Plum as he helped himself to a baked spud.

"I'd told you I'd wring your neck if you cut ahead of me in line!" screamed Mr. Green. He ran to Plum and started wringing away. When Plum slipped to the floor, Green took his potato.

"That roast beef looks delicious," said the female guest who had just helped herself to mashed potatoes. She hurried over and began slicing the roast.

43

Colonel Mustard came back to the Dining Room, wearing a fresh yellow shirt. "I know, I know, you'll challenge me to a duel if you don't get your own way," Scarlet yawned as he took his place in line.

When another guest saw Mustard cut to the head of the line, she became livid. She raced up and grabbed a ladleful of gravy. "Take that, you rude thing!" she cried as she flung it at him.

However, Mustard ducked and the gravy hit the guest behind him. "Ha, ha! The goose gets the gravy!" he laughed in her angry face.

But he wasn't laughing when the next ladleful of gravy hit him. "What's good for the goose is good for the gander!" snapped the prim and proper guest as she threw it at him.

Colonel Mustard took a gander at his gravy-stained shirt. It was the second time that day that he had been hit with food. "I think I'll eat out," he said as he and Scarlet left the line.

Mrs. White approached Mrs. Peacock. "That was pretty funny," she said. "And so is this." She picked up a turkey leg and hit Mrs. Peacock with it.

"Not as funny as *this* is," said Mrs. Peacock, hitting Mrs. White over the head with the other turkey leg.

Just then, Scarlet, who changed clothes so often she could do it in the blink of an eye, returned. She wanted revenge against Mrs. Peacock, and threw gravy on her. "Have some of your own medicine," she snarled.

Mrs. Peacock was delighted, because it was the first time she had tasted the gravy, and she found it delicious. "It doesn't taste like medicine at all," she said sweetly. She went back to get some mashed potatoes to put it on.

Meanwhile, Mr. Green was contentedly cutting off piece after piece of ham and munching away.

"I forgot to get some roast beef," said Miss Scarlet, moving to the roast.

Mr. Green suddenly stopped chewing and saw Plum standing by the vegetables. He ran toward him.

Professor Plum armed himself with a stalk of broccoli. Then he decided to drop-kick a carrot instead, but he had no need to worry. "Leave him alone," screeched Mrs. White, brandishing a turkey leg at Mr. Green. Mr. Green was willing to leave Plum alone and go back to his ham.

Professor Plum forgot his rolls and went to get them.

Mrs. White went back for more scalloped potatoes.

Mr. Boddy came back.

WHAT ORDER ARE THE GUESTS IN NOW?

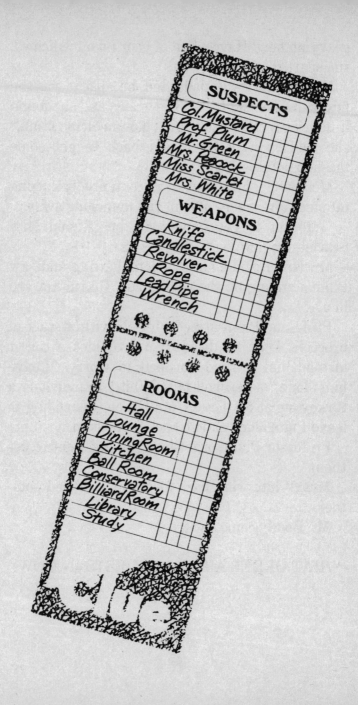

SOLUTION

PROFESSOR PLUM, MRS. WHITE, MRS. PEACOCK, MR. GREEN, and MISS SCARLET

We know that the food was laid out on the table in this order: fruit, appetizers, rolls, scalloped potatoes, mashed potatoes, baked potatoes, ham, roast beef, turkey, gravy, broccoli, spinach, carrots, angel food cake, chocolate cake. By keeping that in mind, we can keep track of the guests' positions as they change places. When Mr. Boddy arrived, Professor Plum was near the rolls, followed by White at the scalloped potatoes, Peacock at the mashed potatoes, Green at the ham, and Scarlet at the roast beef. Colonel Mustard was eating out.

7.
A Bird in the Hand

THE GUESTS WERE SITTING IN THE Conservatory when Mrs. Peacock flew in, wearing a new piece of jewelry. At her neck was a brooch shaped like a bird made of gold and diamonds.

Miss Scarlet, with her eagle eyes, spied it at once. "How much is that brooch worth, if I might broach the subject?"

"Why, how rude!" said Mrs. Peacock. Then she smiled. "But I don't mind telling you that this pin is worth half a million dollars."

"That's the perfect jewel for her," whispered Colonel Mustard to Professor Plum. "I always thought she was a real pin in the neck."

"I always thought she was a real pin in the neck," echoed Professor Plum.

Colonel Mustard jumped to his feet. "Don't parrot what I say, or I'll challenge you to a duel!" he roared.

"Calm down, everyone, said Mr. Boddy. He turned to Mrs Peacock. "Where did you get that lovely piece of jewelry?"

"It was a gift from my cousin, Robin," said Mrs.

Peacock. She glared at the guests. "Don't any of you vultures think of robbin' it." She was glad she had the Revolver with her in case any of the cagey guests tried. Every guest in the room was watching her like a hawk.

"I'll give a party so that you can show it off," said Mr. Boddy.

"Please, not tonight, Mr. Boddy. I've been flying around so much today that I need a rest. I want to have a quiet evening reading my book, *The Fowlest Manners of All.*"

"Well, all right then. I'll give the party another night. You take it easy."

Take it easy, and I'll take that brooch easily, thought a female guest to herself as she remembered the Wrench in her pocket.

"I'll pluck that bird right off your neck," murmured Miss Scarlet to herself as she remembered the weapon she had stashed in her room.

"Stealing that brooch will be a feather in my cap," muttered a male guest. He smiled as he thought of the weapon he had concealed in his jacket.

Half a million bucks isn't chicken feed, the guest who had the Rope was thinking.

The last guest wasn't sure how he was going to steal the brooch, but he was determined to get his hands on it somehow. *I'll just have to wing it,* he thought. *Or maybe I can track it with a bird dog. At least I've got a weapon.*

That night Mrs. Peacock was reading in the
Study when a guest came up behind her, raised
the Candlestick high over his head, and prepared
to strike. Before he could, another guest attacked
him with the Rope.

What's that noise? Mrs. Peacock wondered as a
body fell to the floor.

Why did I do that? the guest with the Rope
asked himself as he looked at the man on the floor.
He totally forgot about the brooch. He left and
went to bed.

"I'll wrench that from your neck," said a guest,
preparing to attack.

"Not so fast," said another guest, who had the
Knife. "I challenge you to a duel!"

I wonder what all the commotion is, Mrs. Peacock thought as they fought behind her chair. "It's
very rude for Mr. Boddy to allow this noise in his
mansion," she sniffed indignantly.

Meanwhile, the two guests behind her chair
were swinging at each other with anything they
could find — their weapons, books, tennis rackets,
shoes, pieces of Genoa salami. Neither guest won.
In the end, they were both unconscious on the
floor.

Now is my chance, thought a guest who had
been watching the whole thing. The guest almost

messed it up when her weapon fell from her hands and rolled across the floor, but she quickly retrieved it and used it to attack Mrs. Peacock and steal her rare bird.

WHO STOLE MRS. PEACOCK'S BROOCH?

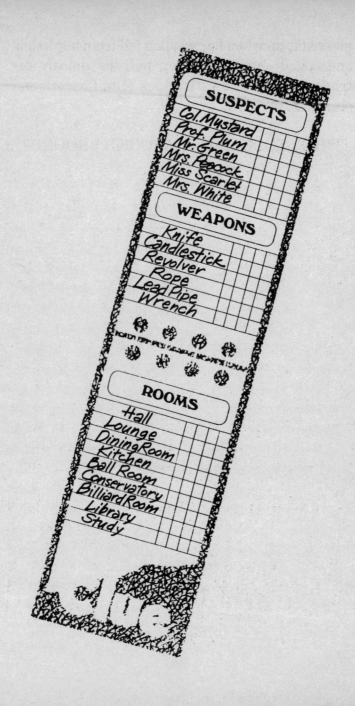

SOLUTION

MISS SCARLET

We know that Mrs. Peacock had the Revolver. The forgetful guest with the Rope was Professor Plum. The man he attacked must have been Mr. Green, who had the Candlestick, since later Colonel Mustard challenged someone to a duel with the Knife. A female guest with the Wrench wants to wrench the brooch from Mrs. Peacock's neck. That must be Mrs. White. Miss Scarlet with the Lead Pipe stole the brooch.

However, soon after the theft, Mr. Boddy thought Miss Scarlet was acting suspiciously. When he questioned her, she sang like a canary. After her confession, he made her clean all the bird cages in the mansion and eat crow. The other guests survived the incident with only minor cuts, bruises, and bumps on the head.

8.
Autograph Hounds

"IT'S RAINING!" EXCLAIMED PROFESsor Plum with amazement as he looked out the window of the Study. It had been raining all day, but Plum kept forgetting. He announced the fact again each time he looked out the window.

The guests had spent the day exploring the mansion. Now they were sitting around thinking about their discoveries and how they could use their new knowledge in committing crimes.

Mrs. White twirled the Candlestick as she thought about the new secret passage she had discovered between the Billiard Room and the Kitchen.

Professor Plum rolled the Lead Pipe in his hands as he thought about the secret passage he had discovered between the Billiard Room and the Lounge.

Mrs. Peacock braided and unbraided the Rope as she thought about the secret passage she had discovered between the Lounge and the Ball Room.

Mr. Green flipped the Wrench as he thought about the secret passage he had discovered between the Ball Room and the Hall.

Miss Scarlet smirked as she toyed with the Knife, because she had watched Mrs. White find a new secret passage, and now she knew about it, too.

Colonel Mustard thought about the Revolver he had stashed in his room, and how surprised Green would be if he showed up in Mr. Green's newly discovered secret passage and challenged him to a duel.

Mr. Boddy appeared in the doorway. "Please accompany me to the Ball Room," he said. "I want to show you a very special treasure."

The guests' eyes gleamed with anticipation as they followed their host. They were all sure that they would soon get the chance to put their knowledge to work.

When they arrived in the Ball Room, Mr. Boddy led them to a wall where he had mounted his latest acquisition. The guests were thrilled.

"Why, it's the autograph of famous composer and musician Nohands Sebastian Bach!" they said in a chorus.

"That's right," Mr. Boddy said, beaming with pride. Then the smile left his face. "It's worth a great deal of money, too. Don't even think about stealing it. Please note that the moment it's found missing, I'll have every one of your rooms searched. Just be sharp and keep your hands off Nohands."

The guests didn't pay any attention. If Mr. Boddy planned to search their rooms, they would simply hide the treasure somewhere else and retrieve it later. Each was certain he or she could capture the prize.

Mrs. Peacock was especially eager to have the autograph. Her mother loved Bach. She couldn't wait to say, "Look, Ma, Nohands!"

"We should have the piano fixed and play some of Bach's music," said Mr. Boddy. "Does anyone know how to tune a piano?"

"Did you say tuna?" asked Professor Plum.

"Don't be ridiculous," snapped Green. "You can tune a piano, but you can't tune a fish."

"Oh, dear," said Mr. Boddy. "I think that last remark gave me a headache. I'm afraid I'll have to lie down for a while."

Later ...

Later, a guest crept softly to the Ball Room, took the autograph from the wall, hid it under his coat, and entered a secret passage. He didn't hide the autograph very well, though. When he emerged from the secret passage in the Hall, a guest spotted him carrying it, attacked him with the Lead Pipe, and knocked him unconscious.

The guest with the Lead Pipe took the autograph and ran into the Lounge. *I'll be in the Billiard Room in no time, and I can hide it under the snooker table*, he thought. Unfortunately, the guest forgot how to get through the secret passage, and he had to turn back halfway and return to the Lounge. There, a guest attacked him with the Rope and took the autograph.

The lady who now had the autograph used the secret passage she had discovered in the Lounge and moments later emerged in the room at the other end. "I'll put this in my hiding place behind these curtains," she whispered. But she was so excited about getting her hands on the autograph that she didn't realize she wasn't whispering at all, but screaming at the top of her lungs. A guest heard her and came rushing into the Ball Room. She attacked her with the Knife and stole the autograph.

Then the guest ran into the Kitchen and entered a secret passage. She was halfway through it when she met another guest. The guest attacked her and took the autograph.

"I know just where to hide this," chuckled the guest as she carried the autograph through the mansion. However, she never got a chance to hide it. She was surprised by the guest with the Revolver.

"I know a perfect hiding place in the Hall," he said to himself as he snatched the autograph. "I'll just use the secret passage and be there in no time."

WHO STOLE THE AUTOGRAPH? WHERE?
WITH WHAT WEAPON?

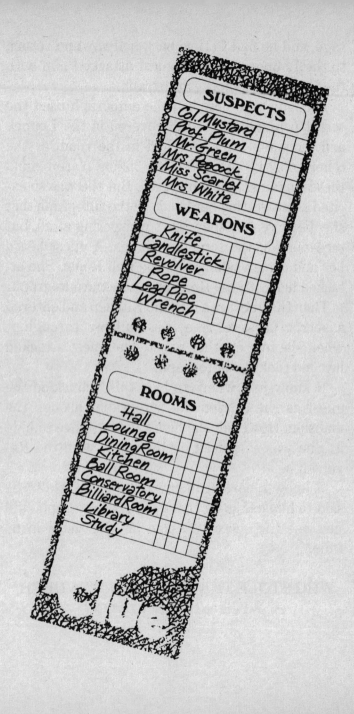

SOLUTION

COLONEL MUSTARD in the BALL ROOM
with the REVOLVER

We know that two guests knew about the secret passage between the Ball Room and the Hall. However, Colonel Mustard has the Revolver. If he planned to hide the autograph in the room he knew was at the other end of the secret passage, he must have been standing in the Ball Room.

Fortunately, none of the guests were seriously injured. The secret passages were full of trick mirrors, and no one could see straight to hurt anyone else.

9.
Trading Cards

"**W**HAT DO YOU HAVE THERE, MR. Boddy?" asked Mrs. White.

The guests formed a semicircle around Mr. Boddy, who was unwrapping some objects and placing them in the china closet in the Dining Room. They craned their necks, trying to see what sort of objects they were.

"Stand back, please, and I'll show you what I have," Mr. Boddy instructed.

When the guests moved away, Mr. Boddy stood up and placed the last object in the closet. "I have just acquired a priceless collection of glass vases that belonged to the king of the Republic of Twaddle."

The guests gasped. It was well known that the king of Twaddle was a collector of only the most valuable items. All of the guests were collectors, too — of anything expensive that wasn't nailed down.

Mr. Boddy stepped aside to let the guests have a look at the vases. They were exquisite, each with a different pattern in the glass — stars, swirls, stripes, dots, flowers, and squares.

Each guest took an instant liking to one of the vases. They also hated every other one.

"The vase with the stars is clearly the most valuable," said Miss Scarlet with authority.

"That just shows your lack of taste," sniffed Mrs. Peacock. "The one with the swirl pattern is clearly worth more than the others."

"Did you say squirrel pattern?" asked Professor Plum. "I don't see any squirrels."

"The only one who is squirrelly around here is *you*," said Mr. Green. "And the only vase worth anything is the striped glass."

"Speaking of glass, did I ever tell you folks that I have a glass jaw?" asked Professor Plum.

"Who cares?" roared Colonel Mustard. "Pick your favorite vase, or I'll challenge you to a duel!"

"Dot's it! The one with the dots!" stammered Plum.

"Are you dotty?" asked Mrs. White, scowling. Then a dreamy look came into her eyes. "The one with the flowers is the most beautiful thing I've ever seen."

"Phooey!" snapped Colonel Mustard. "The only one worth having is the one with the squares."

Mr. Boddy stroked his chin thoughtfully. "It's plain to see that each one of you has a favorite vase and hates all the others. If a vase is missing, I'll know exactly who stole it."

Mr. Boddy folded his arms across his chest. "I want each of you to promise faithfully that you will confess to stealing your favorite vase if you do it."

The guests all promised, although Mrs. White crossed her fingers behind her back. Mr. Boddy caught her and made her promise with them uncrossed.

Later . . .

Later, Miss Scarlet called a meeting in the Study. "I know how to get around those silly promises we made to Mr. Boddy," she said. "He'll never suspect any one of us — if we all steal a vase we don't like. We didn't promise to confess to that, either. Then we'll exchange vases later."

Everyone agreed that Miss Scarlet had a great idea. Miss Scarlet was proud of herself, too. "Just write your favorite pattern on a card," she said. "Then we'll all trade cards."

Professor Plum looked confused. "I thought we wanted to collect vases, not trading cards. I don't like trading cards."

"She didn't say trading cards, you ninny!" snapped Mrs. White.

"I think she's trying to trick us into trading our cars," said Mr. Green slyly. "She's not going to get away with it, either."

"Stop this nonsense!" shrieked Miss Scarlet. She passed out index cards. The guests got down to business and wrote their favorite patterns on the cards.

Then they all traded cards. Scarlet changed with Mustard, Peacock changed with White, and Plum changed with Green. But everyone hated the pattern that he or she got so much that they couldn't even stand to steal it. So they decided to have a second round of exchanges.

White changed with Plum, Mustard changed with Green, and Peacock changed with Scarlet. After the second round, they still hated what they had received and decided to change a third time. Scarlet changed with Plum, Peacock changed with Mustard, and Green changed with White. Now some of them still hated what they got, but Mustard and Green had their own patterns.

They decided to have a fourth round of changes. They shuffled the cards, threw them up in the air, and turned on the electric fan to blow them around the room. At the end of the fourth round, Scarlet was holding White's second-round card, Peacock was holding the card she received in the first round of exchanges, Green was holding Scarlet's third-round card, Plum was holding Peacock's second-round card, White had Mustard's second-round card, and Mustard had the card he received during the first round of trades. They still hated what they had, but decided to live with it. Then, each went and stole a vase.

WHO STOLE WHICH VASE?

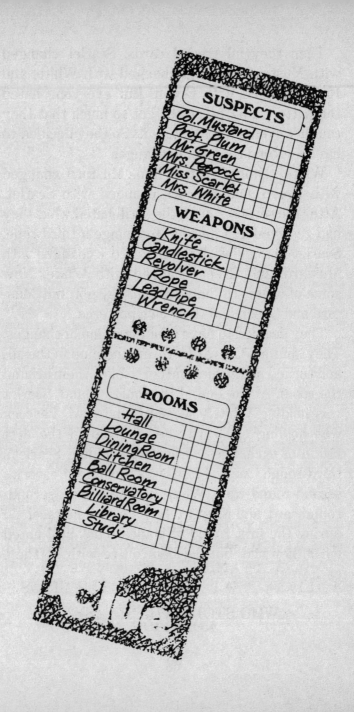

SUSPECTS

Col. Mustard
Prof. Plum
Mr. Green
Mrs. Pecock
Miss Scarlet
Mrs. White

WEAPONS

Knife
Candlestick
Revolver
Rope
Lead Pipe
Wrench

ROOMS

Hall
Lounge
Dining Room
Kitchen
Ball Room
Conservatory
Billiard Room
Library
Study

Clue

SOLUTION

SCARLET stole the striped vase, PEACOCK took the flowered one, GREEN took the swirls, PLUM stole the one with squares, WHITE stole the dotted one, and MUSTARD took the one with stars.

By keeping track of the exchanges, we know that after round one, Scarlet had the squares card, Peacock had the flowers, Green had the dots, Plum had the stripes, White had the swirls, and Mustard had the stars.

After round two, Scarlet had the flowers, Peacock had the squares, Green had the stars, Plum had the swirls, White had the stripes, and Mustard had the dots.

After round three, Scarlet had the swirls, Peacock had the dots, Green had the stripes, Plum had the flowers, White had the stars, and Mustard had the squares.

When Mr. Boddy saw that the vases were missing, he searched the guests' rooms and discovered what they had done. When he confronted them with their thefts, they all gave back the treasures. They were so embarrassed that they couldn't save vase — er, face.

10.
The Vanishing Vampire

Mr. BODDY HAD SENT EACH GUEST AN engraved invitation to come to the Hall in the evening to view his newest treasure. Just outside the entrance, on the wall opposite the staircase, he had hung a picture of a coffin in a graveyard. It was ablaze with light from several spotlights.

Mrs. Peacock was the first to arrive. She stood on the first step at the bottom of the stairway and stared at the painting. She thought it was dreadful and improper, but perhaps worth stealing.

Colonel Mustard was the next to arrive. He stood on the third step. When another guest arrived and tried to stand next to him, Colonel Mustard challenged the guest to a duel.

Here we go again, thought the guest as he moved up to the fourth step.

Mrs. White arrived and stood on the floor in front of Mrs. Peacock. Mrs. Peacock made such a scene that Mrs. White moved up and stood on the step directly below Colonel Mustard. Another guest stepped up beside her.

"You can't stand here," said Mrs. White. "This step is mine."

"I don't see your name on it," the other guest observed, and would not move.

Another male guest arrived and stood on the fifth step.

The guests stood on the stairs and stared, wondering how valuable the painting was and how they could steal it as they clutched their weapons behind their backs.

The female guest on the first step clutched the Revolver.

The female guest who had arrived first on the second step held the Candlestick.

The guest beside her had the Wrench.

The guest above them gripped the Knife.

The male guest above him clasped the Rope.

The male guest above him had the Lead Pipe.

"Say, I've seen that old picture lying around the mansion," said Mr. Green. "Why haven't you hung it sooner?"

"I was waiting for my personal picture hanger, Tooloose Lautrec."

Mrs. White gaped at Mr. Boddy. "But when Tooloose hangs a picture, it always falls off the wall!" she exclaimed.

"That's true," Mr. Boddy said patiently. "However, his partner, Vincent Van Glue, always puts things right."

"Didn't I hear that the two partners had moved to Alabama?" asked Mrs. Peacock.

"Quite right," answered Colonel Mustard before Mr. Boddy could reply. "Since they arrived, the elephants there have been having trouble with their tusks getting loose and falling out."

Professor Plum nodded sagely. "Yes, I've heard about Tuscaloosa, Alabama."

"It doesn't matter," said Mr. Boddy, eager to get back to talking about the painting. "The elephants get their tusks replaced for free at the Tusk-hee-hee Institute. Now please pay attention while I tell you about this painting."

"I'm all ears," said Professor Plum, who had just learned how to wiggle his ears.

"Stop wiggling your ears!" Mr. Boddy snapped. He proceeded to explain that the painting had been found in a crumbling old castle, and was recognized as the *Portrait of a Vanishing Vampire*. Boddy had arranged to sell it to a museum for a lot of money. Meanwhile, he warned the guests that the painting must be well-lit at all times.

"If darkness falls upon the painting of the coffin, the legend says that something terrible will happen," he said gravely.

"I'll bite!" shouted Colonel Mustard. "What would happen?"

"In darkness, the Vanishing Vampire will emerge from the coffin and go on a feeding frenzy," Mr. Boddy said solemnly.

The guests scoffed at the legend. They were sure that Mr. Boddy just wanted to trick them out of stealing the painting.

"Where are you going to put the money you get for it?" asked Miss Scarlet. "In a blood bank?"

"That's right!" said Mrs. White, giving her a playful poke in the ribs. "Because it's blood money!"

This caused general hilarity. The guests all laughed and patted each other on the back. Then they laughed some more. They laughed until they hiccuped and tears were streaming down their faces. Then something happened that made them stop laughing.

"I'm scared!" blurted a guest. "I'm terrified of vampires, and I'm frightened of that awful painting!" It was Professor Plum. The guests all stared as he ran shrieking from the room.

I'm scared, too, thought another guest, but didn't mention it to anyone.

That night . . .

That night, when the mansion was dark, a guest used the Revolver to pry the painting from the wall. She took it and ran into the Study. There, she stopped to catch her breath. *Thank goodness no one saw me,* she thought.

But someone did. Another guest followed her, attacked her with the Knife, and took the painting.

"It's mine!" he whispered joyfully as he ran into the Library.

"I don't think so," he heard a voice say behind him just before he was hit over the head with the Lead Pipe. The guest with the Lead Pipe tucked the painting underneath his arm and began walking through the mansion. He hadn't gone far when he was confronted by another guest. In the darkness, all he could see was the gleaming Wrench. The two guests peered at each other, unable to see clearly.

Finally the guest with the Wrench burst out, "I know who you are! What are you doing with that painting? You're terrified of the vampire in the coffin!"

The guest with the painting had forgotten this. He suddenly realized that he was indeed afraid. He dropped the painting and raced away.

The guest with the Wrench picked it up and groped through the mansion in the darkness. *"Boddy will go batty when he finds out the painting has been stolen,"* she chuckled.

While she was chuckling, the guest with the Wrench was attacked by the guest with the Rope. They stumbled and banged into each other as they tried to fight in the dark. Finally, the guest with the Wrench whirled around suddenly, unable to see the other guest — or anything else — then banged into the wall and was knocked out.

The guest with the Rope barely had time to

enjoy his good fortune. Mr. Boddy had gotten out of bed for a midnight snack and heard the commotion. Soon he was shining the light from his flashlight in the guest's face. He ripped the painting from the guest's hands. "You'll take this painting over my dead body!" he shouted.

"Fine, if that's the way you want it!" The guest sprang at him and twisted the Rope around his neck. After a moment Mr. Boddy was a dead Boddy.

Just then, the guest with the Rope heard a strange noise like the flapping of a bird's wings — or a bat's. He gripped the garlic he had hung around his neck earlier and turned slowly. In the light of the full moon coming through the window, he could see a figure with long, pointed fangs wrapped in a huge cape. The vampire!

Terror-stricken, the guest was unable to move. The vampire grabbed the garlic and hissed. "Great! I can use this to make a pizza." Then the vampire sank its fangs into the guest's neck.

WHO KILLED MR. BODDY?/WITH WHAT WEAPON?

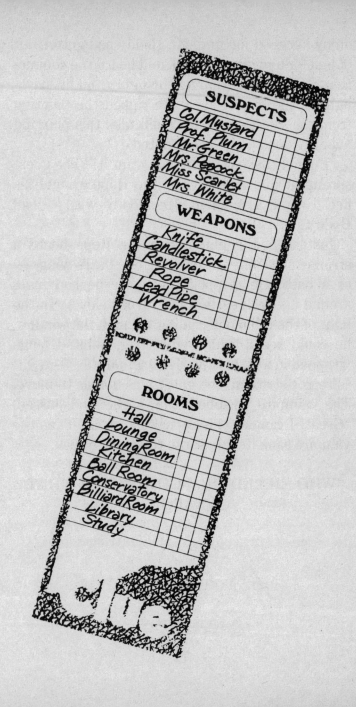

SOLUTION

MR. GREEN with the ROPE

By keeping track of where each guest stood on the staircase, we can find out what weapon each one had. Mrs. Peacock had the Revolver, Mrs. White had the Candlestick, and Colonel Mustard had the Knife. The guest who forgot he was scared was Professor Plum with the Lead Pipe. By process of elimination, we know that the remaining male guest was Mr. Green with the Rope, and the remaining female guest was Miss Scarlet with the Wrench. Mrs. White, who had the Candlestick, was afraid to try to steal the painting.

Everyone besides Mr. Boddy was unharmed. It was so dark in the mansion that all of the guests' aims were way off. Mr. Green was a victim of his own overactive imagination. He wasn't attacked by a vampire at all — just someone with unusual teeth and a strange fashion sense. It was Boddy's cousin, Bitsy Boddy, who decided to play a prank on the guests.

Get a clue...
Your favorite board game is a mystery series!

by A.E. Parker

Who killed Mr. Boddy? Was it Mrs. Peacock in the Library with the Revolver?
Or Professor Plum in the Ballroom with the Knife? If you Like Playing the
game, you'll love solving the mini-mysteries in these great books!

☐ BAM46110-9	#1	Who Killed Mr. Boddy?	$3.50
☐ BAM45631-8	#2	The *Secret* Secret Passage	$2.99
☐ BAM45632-6	#3	The Case of the Invisible Cat	$2.95
☐ BAM45633-4	#4	Mystery at the Masked Ball	$2.95
☐ BAM47804-4	#5	Midnight Phone Calls	$3.25
☐ BAM47805-2	#6	Booby Trapped	$3.50
☐ BAM48735-3	#7	The Picture Perfect Crime	$3.25
☐ BAM48934-8	#8	The Clue in the Shadow	$3.25
☐ BAM48935-6	#9	Mystery in the Moonlight	$3.50
☐ BAM48936-4	#10	The Screaming Skeleton	$3.50
☐ BAM62374-5	#11	Death by Candlelight	$3.50
☐ BAM62375-3	#12	The Haunted Gargoyle	$3.50
☐ BAM62376-1	#13	The Revenge of the Mummy	$3.50
☐ BAM62377-X	#14	The Dangerous Diamond	$3.50

Scholastic Inc., P.O. Box 7502, 2931 East McCarty Street, Jefferson City, MO 65102

Please send me the books I have checked above. I am enclosing $_____ (please add $2.00 to
cover shipping and handling). Send check or money order—no cash or C.O.D.s please.

Name_____Birthdate_____

Address_____

City_____State/Zip_____

Please allow four to six weeks for delivery. Offer good in U.S. only. Sorry mail orders are not
available to residents of Canada. Prices subject to change.   CL396